SUPER DC HEROES

BATMAN

THE PUPPET MASTER'S REVENGE

WRITTEN BY
DONALD LEMKE

ILLUSTRATED BY
**RICK BURCHETT AND
LEE LOUGHRIDGE**

BATMAN CREATED BY
BOB KANE

STONE ARCH BOOKS
MINNEAPOLIS   SAN DIEGO

Published by Stone Arch Books in 2010
151 Good Counsel Drive, P.O. Box 669
Mankato, Minnesota 56002
www.stonearchbooks.com

Library of Congress Cataloging-in-Publication Data

Lemke, Donald
  The puppet master's revenge / by Donald Lemke ; illustrated by Rick
Burchett.
     p. cm. -- (DC super heroes. Batman)
  ISBN 978-1-4342-1560-4 (lib. bdg.) -- ISBN 978-1-4342-1727-1 (pbk.)
  [1. Superheroes--Fiction.] I. Burchett, Rick, ill. II. Title.
  PZ7.L53746Pu 2010
  [Fic]--dc22
                                        2009008736

Summary: The evil puppet Scarface and his wiseguys just pulled off one
of the biggest heists in Gotham history. But, there's a rat among the
thieves, and the loose lips are helping Batman crack the case. Has the
Ventriloquist betrayed his wooden creation to the Dark Knight?

Art Director: Bob Lentz
Designer: Brann Garvey

Printed in the United States of America

TABLE OF CONTENTS

CHAPTER 1

PUPPET HEIST

Three minutes past midnight, a small cargo plane touched down at Gotham International Airport. Near the main gate, a security officer stepped out of his armored truck. He had waited more than an hour for the shipment to arrive.

"Hurry it up, boys!" shouted the guard.

Two ground crew workers stood a few feet away, chuckling. They warmed their hands near the engine of a forklift. Both wore thick coveralls, blue vests, and oversized headsets.

One had a gray ski mask pulled over his face to protect against the cold. "You got it," he growled. The worker spit a chewed up toothpick onto the ground and mumbled toward his partner. Then he jumped into the cab of the forklift.

Soon, the plane's rear door opened like a mechanical jaw. A metal ramp unfolded like its tongue. Steam from the heated cargo bay filled the November air.

Eighteen hours earlier in the Czech Republic, a large wooden crate marked *Národní Muzeum* had been loaded onto the plane. It contained some of the Prague National Museum's rarest pieces of artwork, including two ancient sculptures and three Bohemian paintings. The crate also contained a 200-year-old marionette — one of the oldest puppets in the world.

"The one near the back," said the guard. He pointed inside the cargo bay at the wooden crate. "Be careful! It's worth more than your life."

The man in the ski mask stopped the forklift near the ramp. "Is it worth more than *yours*?" he asked. Then he sped into the plane before the guard could answer.

The guard turned to the other worker. "What's that supposed to mean?" he asked.

"Ha ha ha!" The other worker stood at the end of the ramp. He was laughing wildly, snorting like a pig.

"You think that's funny?" questioned the guard. He grabbed a walkie-talkie from his belt. "Wait until your boss finds out!"

"For some reason," the worker said with a smile, "I don't think he'd mind!"

VROOOOOM! Suddenly, the guard heard the sound of an engine thundering behind him. He quickly turned and saw the forklift barreling down the ramp. It held the large wooden crate high in the air.

"No!" screamed the guard.

It was too late. The forklift came to a sudden stop, tipping its cargo forward.

SMASH! The giant crate crashed to the ground. Its priceless cargo scattered across the icy ground.

"Look what you've done!" shouted the guard, kneeling next to the pile of exposed paintings and sculptures. "You'll never get away with this!"

"I'm afraid we already have," said the masked worker, hopping out of the forklift.

The worker kneeled down next to the security guard and grabbed the keys from his uniform. "Thanks!" he said.

Then the masked worker scooped up the marionette from the scattered pile and headed toward the armored truck. The other worker followed closely behind.

Before the guard could recover, the crooks had already passed through airport security and escaped into the night.

CHAPTER 2

A HAND IN THE CRIME

An hour later, the Bat-Signal lit up the sky over Gotham City. At the edge of the city, the armored truck turned into an alleyway on Murphy Avenue. Behind the Donnegan Saloon, an unmarked storage garage slowly opened for its arrival.

"It's us, boss," said one of the crooks. He pulled off his mask, stepped out of the truck and into the darkened garage.

"I can see that, Nicky," replied a voice from the shadows. "What do I look like, a dummy?"

The other thug let out a snort. "Ha! Good one, boss," he said.

"You think that's some kind of a joke, wiseguy?" said the angered voice. "Let me ask you again." Suddenly, Scarface burst out of the darkness. The evil puppet wore a pinstripe suit and a fedora hat. He had an evil grin on his wooden face. "Do I look like a dummy?"

"No, sir, Scarface, sir," squealed the crook. "I wasn't making fun of your, I mean, I didn't mean to —"

"Shut your trap, Harvey, before I shut it for you," shouted Scarface. The man controlling the puppet remained hidden in the shadow. "Now where's the goods?"

Nicky quickly reached into the front seat of the armored truck.

Then he turned back around and held the Czech marionette in the air. Except for a few smudges, the 200-year-old puppet hadn't been damaged in the fall.

"Rosalie," whispered Scarface. He reached his wooden hand toward the marionette. He touched its white, porcelain cheek and stroked the long blond hair. "Just as I had imagined."

Six months earlier, the *Gotham Gazette* newspaper had reported that the marionette, nicknamed Rosalie, would be displayed at the Gotham City Museum. Scarface had studied the puppet ever since. He read about her history in the Czech theater, her delicate ceramic face, and her hand-sewn dress. More importantly, he learned that the marionette was estimated to be worth more than $50 million.

Now, however, Scarface felt drawn by something more powerful than a quick payday. "She stays," he said, taking the marionette in his arms.

"But, but, sir —" For the first time that night, Scarface's mild-mannered ventriloquist stepped out from the shadows. Of the many voices that swirled in Arnold Wesker's insane head, Scarface was the one he never questioned. "But sir," the Ventriloquist continued. "I don't think we should —"

"That's right, dummy!" Scarface snapped at his puppet master. "You don't think, and let's keep it that way."

"What about our cut?" snorted Harvey. "I mean, you owe us ten percent of the take. That's fifty grand."

With a quick tip of his head, Scarface directed the Ventriloquist to move him closer to the crooks. His cool, glassy eyes stared at them violently.

"You know, Harvey, you're right," said Scarface. His voice sounded surprisingly less angry.

Harvey stood up straight. "I am?" he asked, snickering with relief.

"Yeah," Scarface replied. "Hold out your hand so I can give you what you deserve."

Harvey glanced over at Nicky. His partner chomped nervously on a toothpick, and didn't offer any advice.

"Hold out your hand!" Scarface shouted.

Harvey hesitated for another moment. Then he raised his shaky palm into the air toward the evil puppet.

Scarface's wooden jaw snapped down on the crook's fingers. Moments later, the puppet released his fierce grip.

"Yeeooooww!" cried Harvey, holding his crumpled fist.

"Don't ever tell me what to do!" Scarface shouted at the fearful crooks. "I'm the boss around here! Now get out! Both of you!"

"Yes, sir, Mr. Scarface, sir," said Harvey, scrambling toward the armored truck.

"Yeah, you're the boss," repeated Nicky, following his partner.

As the crooks sped out of the garage, Scarface held the marionette in the air. He looked toward the Ventriloquist. "Now, let's find a place for my lovely Rosalie," he said.

Back at the airport, Commissioner Jim Gordon and the Gotham City Police had arrived at the scene. For more than an hour, officers searched the scene for clues and questioned the security guard. So far, they weren't having any luck with the case.

"Where's Batman?" asked Gordon, pacing back and forth. He stared down at the damaged artwork. "I signaled him more than an hour ago."

"I'd say forty-five minutes," a deep voice came from behind.

Gordon turned and spotted Batman. He was kneeling a few feet away, rubbing the ground with his thick black gloves.

"When did you get here?" asked Gordon.

"I've been investigating the airport security," replied the Dark Knight.

"And?" asked the Commissioner. "How does it check out?"

"I'm here, aren't I?" said Batman, looking up from the icy ground.

The commissioner walked toward the Dark Knight. He popped the collar of his trench coat and blew into his nearly frozen hands. "So the security isn't top-notch," he said, shrugging his shoulders. "I've got two half-naked and half-frozen ground crew workers who can testify to that."

Batman glanced up at the commissioner.

"Yeah," Gordon continued. "Found them tied up in a baggage cart three gates away. The crooks stole their uniforms and left them for dead. Neither victim got a good look at the thieves, but the guard says one snorted like a pig."

"And the prize?" asked Batman.

The commissioner glanced back at the pieces of art near the shattered crate. The officers had covered the scene with a blue tarp, trying to preserve the remains of the damaged goods.

"A big one," replied Gordon. "A 200-year-old Czech marionette nicknamed Rosalie. It's worth nearly $50 million."

"If you can get rid of it," added Batman. "If anyone tries to sell that thing on the black market, they'll get pinched for sure."

"Right," continued Gordon. "So who would risk twenty to life in the slammer for a doll he can't sell?"

Batman stood and extended his gloved fist toward Gordon. Between his fingers, he held the butt of a frayed toothpick.

"Nicky the Pick?" questioned the commissioner. He grabbed the used toothpick from Batman's hand and studied it closer.

"With a little help from Hog-faced Harvey, I'd say," said Batman.

"But those guys are thugs," said Gordon. "My boys picked them up last month for knocking over a penny arcade. Someone else had a hand in this heist."

Batman turned and began to walk away. "You know, Commissioner," he added. "I think you might be right."

CHAPTER 3

INSANELY JEALOUS

Two nights later at the Donnegan Saloon, Scarface settled into a tall, leather chair inside his private office. The room was filled with dozens of stolen objects including diamond rings, fur coats, and expensive cigars. All of the items would eventually make their way to the black market — all except one.

The priceless marionette, Rosalie, rested limply next to Scarface. Ever since the robbery, she had never left his side.

"She can't stay," said the Ventriloquist.

The Ventriloquist sat on the other side of the room, staring at his cold, naked hand. "You said yourself it's too risky," he said.

"Don't put words in my mouth!" shouted Scarface. "You're just jealous, aren't you?"

"No, sir, but what about the plan?" started the Ventriloquist. "What if the police — ?"

"Stop whining!" shouted the evil puppet. "I'm the one made of wood, but you're the one acting like a sap. The police haven't got a thing on us. Those bumbling fools couldn't catch a cold."

BANG! BANG! BANG! A loud pounding came from outside the office door. Scarface didn't move. He sat stiffly behind the desk, knowing that his trusty Thompson machine gun was hidden underneath.

"What should I do, sir?" asked the Ventriloquist, shaking with fright.

BANG! BANG! BANG! The pounding came again.

"Well, open it, dummy," replied Scarface. "Slowly."

The Ventriloquist placed his ear to the door for a moment and listened. Then he unlocked three steel dead bolts and unhooked a chain from the doorframe.

CRASH! Two men burst through the door. They fumbled over each other and fell to the floor in a heap.

"Boss, you gotta help us!" cried Nicky the Pick, groveling on his knees. Tears and sweat ran down his dirty face. His clothes hadn't been changed in the past two days. "He's after us, sir."

"Who?" questioned Scarface. "You're lucky you didn't get shot bursting in here."

"That's better than what he'll do to us," whimpered Harvey. "Batman! He knows we're behind the heist."

"Where did you hear that?" asked the Ventriloquist.

"Shut it! He's talking to me," shouted Scarface toward his puppeteer. "Now, where did you get that information?"

"Where? It's all over the news, boss," said Nicky, wiping sweat from his brow. "I'm a dead man walkin'."

"Calm down and listen," Scarface said. "Let me tell you what you're gonna do."

The two crooks crawled across the office floor. They kneeled next to their boss's chair and groveled at the evil puppet's feet.

"Anything, boss! Anything you ask!" they sobbed.

"Get out of here!" Scarface shouted at the cowering thugs. "I don't need this heat coming down on me!"

"But, boss —" began Nicky.

"And another thing," continued Scarface. "You mention my name to anyone, and Batman will be the least of your worries. I don't take kindly to rats, if you know what I mean. Now get out!"

Nicky and Harvey lifted themselves off the floor. They scrambled backward out of the door, afraid to turn their backs on the evil puppet.

As they left, the Ventriloquist turned back toward Scarface.

"You too!" shouted Scarface.

"Me?" asked the Ventriloquist, startled by the puppet's request.

"Get out!" Scarface replied. "Leave me alone . . . with Rosalie."

The Ventriloquist glared angrily at the 200-year-old puppet. Even as an orphaned boy, he had never felt so rejected by another. Without a word, the puppet master turned and left the room, a glimmer of hatred in his eyes.

CHAPTER 4

HONOR AMONG THIEVES

Meanwhile, the Dark Knight sped through the heart of Gotham in the Batmobile. For the past three days, he had searched every corner of the city. Still, he had found no leads on the suspects.

Suddenly, a light on the Batmobile's dashboard lit up, signaling an incoming call. "Activate phone," he commanded.

"This is Commissioner Gordon," said a voice on the other end. "I have a real nutcase on the line. Says he's got info on the heist, but he refuses to give his name."

"Patch him through, Commissioner," replied Batman.

The dashboard light signaled that the call had been transferred, but Batman heard nothing but silence. "Hello?" he inquired. "You have information on the Rosalie case?"

For a brief moment, the man didn't reply. "I won't let him treat me like this," the shaky voice began. "I've stood behind him long enough."

"Who?" asked Batman. This was the evidence he needed. "Who are you protecting?"

"A black SUV. No plates. Heading west on Rice Street," said the man, refusing to answer the question. "That's all I can say. What have I done?!"

Suddenly, the light on the dashboard blinked off and the caller was gone. Without hesitating, Batman cranked the steering wheel to the right. The Batmobile spun around on the icy pavement.

Batman switched on the Batmobile's afterburners. With a sudden jolt, the car reached maximum speed. "Looks like something, or someone, is starting to break," said Batman, speeding through the streets of downtown Gotham City.

Moments later, he was right on the tail of the black SUV. It swerved in and out of traffic, careened over a sidewalk, and nearly hit a pedestrian. Soon the SUV had reached the entrance to the Trigate Bridge.

"He's heading out of Gotham City," Batman muttered. "Time for this little joyride to end."

Batman picked up speed and followed closely behind. Then he hit a switch on the dashboard. Rockets fired, and the Batmobile suddenly shot forward, pulling up beside the SUV.

As Batman suspected, Nicky the Pick was sitting in the front seat. Alongside him sat Hog-faced Harvey, another well-known crook in Gotham. Batman gave a quick wave and a knowing smirk. Then he pressed a small red button on the Batmobile's control panel.

With a quick puff of air, a large grappling hook shot out of the side of the Batmobile. The sharp, metal point of the hook pierced the SUV's rubber tire. The SUV squealed and spun, then hit the curb and rammed into the bridge's guardrail.

Batman slammed on his brakes. At the same time, he hit the *retract* button for the grappling hook. The super-strong wire connected to the hook pulled tight, and the SUV quickly came to a stop. It teetered on the edge of the bridge, held safely in place by the wire.

Batman exited the Batmobile and walked toward the SUV. He swung open the door and grabbed Nicky by the collar.

"Who are you working for?" Batman growled at the crook.

Battered from the crash, Nicky stared at the Dark Knight in a daze.

"Who?!" repeated Batman.

Nicky gave a slight smirk. "I don't know what you're talking about," he spat at the Dark Knight.

"All right," Batman said, releasing his grip on Nicky. The Dark Knight bent down and grabbed onto the grappling hook wire that connected the SUV to the Batmobile. "But that water down there looks awfully cold. It'd be a shame if this wire snapped with your partner still inside there."

Nicky stared at the SUV. The passenger door had been crushed, and his pig-nosed partner was trapped inside the vehicle. "You think I'd miss that snorting fool?" replied Nicky. "He got us into this mess!"

"Oh well," said Batman. He pulled out a glittering knife and slowly lowered it onto the cable. The coil of super-strong wire quickly began to fray.

"It was Scarface!" cried Harvey from inside the SUV. "He put us up to it! Now get me out of here!"

"So much for honor among thieves," Batman said to himself.

TWANNNGG! The wire suddenly snapped under the weight of the SUV. With Harvey still inside, the SUV teetered back and forth on the edge of the bridge. Then it suddenly tipped, plunging toward the icy water.

Without a second to lose, Batman grabbed a handheld grapnel gun from his Utility Belt. He aimed it at the falling SUV and fired. **CLANK!** As the hook latched onto the SUV's bumper, Batman wrapped the other end around the bridge rail.

"You didn't think I'd let you get away that easily, did you?" Batman shouted off the edge of the bridge.

Far below, the black SUV dangled safely above the icy water.

CHAPTER 5

TRUE CRIMINAL

Later that evening, a Gotham City SWAT team stormed inside the Donnegan Saloon, searching for Scarface. Instead, they seized box after box of stolen goods, loading them into the trunks of their police cruisers.

A block away, Scarface and the Ventriloquist watched the entire scene unfold through the tinted windows of a silver sedan.

"Drat!" exclaimed Scarface. "How did they track those idiots down so quickly?"

"At least they didn't get Rosalie," continued Scarface. "We'll find a place to keep her safe until this thing dies down."

"But, sir," said the Ventriloquist. "Perhaps, if we get rid of Rosalie —"

"Another word and I'll scar you worse than this," shouted Scarface. The evil puppet pointed to a long, jagged scar down the front of his face. "Now drive!"

Two hours later, the silver sedan pulled up to a small cabin more than a hundred miles outside Gotham. Scarface had used the cabin before as a hideout. He planned to stay there until the heat died down.

"Start a fire," Scarface shouted, as the Ventriloquist carried him and Rosalie into the cabin. "Rosalie is cold. She's as white as a ghost!"

The Ventriloquist set the puppet on an old sofa. He looked at her white, porcelain face, rolled his eyes and then followed his boss's orders.

Soon the fire was ablaze. Scarface sat next to his beloved Rosalie on the sofa. The Ventriloquist paced back and forth across the rug, nervously mumbling to himself.

"What are you whispering, you fool?!" shouted Scarface. "Go fetch some more wood. Rosalie and I want to be alone."

"Yes, sir," said the Ventriloquist. The puppet master grabbed his coat and hat. He let out a long sigh. Then he opened the front door of the cabin.

"Ah!" he exclaimed.

"Batman!" yelled Scarface, recognizing the crime fighter. "How did you find us?"

Batman stepped inside the cabin. He walked slowly toward the evil puppet. "I always thought close friends were 'as thick as thieves,'" replied Batman. "But it seems you boys don't know each other at all."

Batman glanced down at the Ventriloquist. The puppet master scurried backward across the floor. He grabbed Scarface off of the couch and began controlling the puppet in his hand.

Scarface turned toward the Ventriloquist. "What does he mean?" he yelled.

"I don't know," mumbled the Ventriloquist.

"Have you forgotten our conversation already, Wesker?" said Batman, moving closer to the frightened crook. "Let me refresh your memory."

Batman pulled a communicator from his Utility Belt. He opened the tiny recording device and pressed Play. **CLICK!**

". . . I won't let that puppet come between us," Wesker's voice played back from the recorder. "You'll find Rosalie inside the cabin at the end of Pinebrook Road. Scarface will be there as well . . . "

CLICK! Batman stopped the recorder.

"Any other rat wouldn't utter another word," growled Scarface. "But my foolish friend here has done me quite a favor."

"Huh?" questioned the Ventriloquist.

"You see, Batman," continued Scarface. "I've got you right where I want you."

Scarface lifted his fedora. From underneath the hat, the evil puppet snatched a pearl-handled Derringer pistol.

Just as quickly, Batman grabbed a Batarang from his Utility Belt. He drew his arm back, ready to toss the deadly weapon.

"Don't do it, Wesker," Batman shouted. "He doesn't control you."

"Why are you pleading with *him*?" yelled Scarface. "I'm holding the gun!"

"You don't have to listen to him, Wesker," continued Batman. "I know you're in there. I know you're stronger than he is."

Scarface pulled the hammer back on the pistol. "You're wrong," Scarface shouted, shaking the gun toward the Dark Knight. "He's a fool. A dummy. I'm the one in control! And when you're gone, Rosalie and I will be together." Scarface turned the gun toward the Ventriloquist. "And neither of you can stop us."

WHAM! Scarface's wooden head cracked against the back of the fireplace. His body slid into the flames and began to smolder.

On the other side of the room, Batman lowered his Batarang. Arnold Wesker stood next to him, looking dizzy. His eyes were rolling back into his head. Batman quickly grabbed him before he fell to the floor. He led Wesker to the sofa next to Rosalie.

"Thank you, Batman," whispered Wesker, sitting limply on the sofa. "It's finally over."

The Dark Knight grasped Wesker's hand. "It is now," he added, placing a set of batcuffs around the criminal's wrists.

"What?" said Wesker, looking up in shock.

"It was Scarface!" Wesker said. "He was behind the crime. I stopped him! I threw him into the fire!"

"But it *was* you, Wesker," said Batman. "You were behind Scarface all along."

Batman stood and led Wesker toward the door of the cabin. Before he left, Wesker glanced back toward the fire.

Scarface was gone.

Burned, Wesker thought. *Burned to ashes.* He turned and walked through the cabin door. The cold, winter air made him shiver.

Or is he? wondered the Ventriloquist.

Ventriloquist & Scarface

REAL NAME: Arnold Wesker

OCCUPATION: Gang Boss and Puppeteer

BASE: Gotham City

HEIGHT:
5 feet 7 inches

WEIGHT:
142 pounds

EYES:
Blue

HAIR:
Gray

Scarface is one of the most feared criminals in Gotham City's underworld. But Scarface is just a puppet in the hands of the real man in charge, Arnold Wesker. Known as the Ventriloquist, Wesker uses the wooden puppet as an outlet for his violent tendencies. Over time, Scarface came to represent more than just a voice inside Wesker's head — the two sides of his personality constantly battle for control, making it impossible to tell who's really pulling the strings.

G.C.P.D. GOTHAM CITY POLICE DEPARTMENT

- When times get tough, Scarface pulls a Derringer pistol from beneath his trademark fedora hat. The weapon is puppet-sized so that the wooden dummy can hold it himself.

- Wesker once lost his prized dummy, Scarface. Lonely, Wesker found a new puppet — a white sock! He named him Socko, and the two teamed up for a short time. When Scarface returned, the sock and the dummy fought against each other, and Wesker was caught in the crossfire.

- The Ventriloquist specializes in throwing his voice. The Caped Crusader, however, is a master of the technique as well. When Wesker and Scarface had the Dark Knight in danger, Batman used the technique to trick Wesker.

- After Scarface was destroyed, Wesker was imprisoned in Arkham Asylum. He underwent psychological treatment to free himself of his violent alter ego. The therapy seemed to be working — until Wesker was caught carving a new Scarface out of a block of wood.

CONFIDENTIAL

BIOGRAPHIES

Donald Lemke works as a children's book editor. He is the author of the Zinc Alloy graphic novel adventure series. He also wrote *Captured Off Guard*, a World War II story, and a graphic novelization of *Gulliver's Travels*, both of which were selected by the Junior Library Guild.

Rick Burchett has worked as a comics artist for more than 25 years. He has received the comics industry's Eisner Award three times, Spain's Haxtur Award, and he has been nominated for England's Eagle award. Rick lives with his wife and two sons near St. Louis, Missouri.

Lee Loughridge has been working in comics for more than 14 years. He currently lives in sunny California in a tent on the beach.

GLOSSARY

careened (kuh-REEND)—leaned or tipped to the side while in motion

cowering (KOU-ur-ing)—crouching in fear or shame

delicate (DEL-uh-kuht)—easily broken or damaged

fierce (FEERSS)—strong and dangerous

groveled (GROV-uhld)—showed fear and respect by acting unnaturally humble or polite

seized (SEEZD)—arrested or captured something suddenly

shattered (SHAT-urd)—broke into many pieces

Utility Belt (yoo-TIL-uh-tee BELT)—Batman's belt, which holds all of his weaponry and gadgets

DISCUSSION QUESTIONS

1. Should Batman have let Wesker go for helping him find Scarface? Why or why not?

2. Scarface and the Ventriloquist hide in a cabin to escape Batman. If you needed to hide, where would you go?

3. If you were Batman, would you keep your true identity a secret? Why or why not?

WRITING PROMPTS

1. Write another chapter to this book where Scarface survives. Is he looking for revenge? Does he have other plans? You decide.

2. Wesker is scared of Scarface. Have you ever been scared of something or someone? Write about your scary experience.

3. If you were a ventriloquist, what would your puppet look like? Write a brief description of your puppet. Then draw a picture of it.

WAIT!!

DON'T CLOSE THE BOOK!

THERE'S MORE!

FIND MORE:
GAMES & PUZZLES
HEROES & VILLAINS
AUTHORS & ILLUSTRATORS

AT...
www.CAPSTONEKIDS.com

STILL WANT MORE?
FIND COOL WEBSITES AND MORE BOOKS LIKE THIS ONE AT
WWW.FACTHOUND.COM. JUST TYPE IN THE BOOK ID:
1434215601 AND YOU'RE READY TO GO!